BAKERS' DOZEN

#5

OLIVIA AND THE CLASS CREEPS

Suzanne Weyn

A
LITTLE APPLE
PAPERBACK

SCHOLASTIC INC.
New York Toronto London Auckland Sydney

To Diana Weyn Gonzalez

ISBN 0-590-43563-9

Copyright © 1992 by Daniel Weiss Associates, Inc. and Chardiet Unlimited, Inc. All rights reserved. Published by Scholastic Inc. APPLE PAPERBACKS is a registered trademark of Scholastic Inc.

12 11 10 9 8 7 6 5 4 3 2 1   2 3 4 5 6 7/9

Printed in the U.S.A.   28

First Scholastic printing, May 1992

1

Olivia's Space Box

OLIVIA BAKER WOKE UP early on Friday morning. She yawned and ran her fingers through her short, curly brown hair. Then she yawned again.

She shared the large bedroom with two of her sisters. They were still asleep in their bunk beds. Collette was on the bottom bunk. She lay on her side, hugging her pillow. Her long, wavy black hair spread around her dark face like a fan.

Collette was the same age as Olivia. Eight.

Olivia's other sister, Terry, was seven. Her blonde curls dangled down from the top bunk.

Olivia listened. The house was quiet. It was very unusual for the Baker house to be quiet. Very *very* unusual. That was because a lot of people lived there.

Mr. and Mrs. Baker plus their twelve adopted children made fourteen. And Grannie Baker often came for long visits, so sometimes there were fifteen in the house. Plus, there was Jojo, the large, black retriever, who was like a member of the family. Fifteen people and a dog could make a *lot* of noise!

Though it was early — the silver-blue haze of early dawn was just beginning to light the room — Olivia was too excited to go back to sleep. She'd been looking forward to this Friday for a long while. Today she was going to present her science project to the class.

Her project was a very special box filled with carefully chosen objects. The objects were meant to tell people from outer space all about Earth.

She knew this wasn't a crazy idea. Scientists had already sent things like this to outer space. They had sent up a tape recording of whale sounds, and pictures of people. They had included math, and writing in many different languages. The scientists put it all in a space satellite. No one was in the satellite — just the things for the outer space people to find.

Olivia tossed off her blue quilt and sat up. Pulling her flannel nightgown closer to her, she slid off the bed.

A pair of blue-framed eyeglasses sat on her night table. Olivia put them on and gazed up at the poster of Sally Ride that hung over her bed. In the hazy morning light, Sally's face seemed to glow with an inner light of its own.

Olivia pulled back her shoulders and lifted her chin. She smiled, trying to make her top lip straight, like Sally's. She wanted to be like Sally Ride in every way.

Sally Ride was the first American woman to go into outer space, and Olivia idolized her. She had even tried to get her brothers and sisters to call her Sally.

They refused.

"You don't look like Sally Ride," said her seven-year-old brother Howie.

"And you're not an astronaut," six-year-old Kevin added.

"But I will be someday," Olivia told them. There was no doubt in Olivia's mind that one day she would board a spaceship and travel to outer space. "I want to do it so much that it has to happen," she'd say. "It has to."

She would float, weightless, through the starry skies! Walk on the moon! Visit other planets! And one thought thrilled Olivia more than any other.

Someday she might meet people from another planet!

They were out there. She was sure of it.

Sometimes she imagined them as gentle

giants in long, flowing robes. Other times they looked like the sweet, big-eyed creature in *E.T.*, Olivia's favorite outer space movie.

Olivia opened the closet door and slid out a box. It had once contained her sister Christine's new boots. Now it held everything Olivia was putting in her science project. Olivia sat on the floor and opened the box. "Hmmmm," she mused softly. "It needs more stuff."

"Why are you up so early?" mumbled Collette sleepily.

"My project isn't finished yet," Olivia told her. "I'm trying to figure out what else to put in."

Collette got out of bed and joined Olivia on the floor. She reached into the box and picked up the tape she had helped Olivia record. All the Bakers had contributed something.

Their sisters Patty and Hilary sang "We Are the World" on the tape. Mr. Baker, who was a professor, recited a poem. Mrs.

Baker read her recipe for chocolate cake. Grannie Baker yodeled. (She had learned to yodel during a visit to Switzerland.)

Howie had insisted on taping the sound of the toilet flushing. And they recorded Kenny's frog croaking. Jack played his toy drum, and three-year-old Dixie had spoken a few words. *"Goodnight Moon,"* she said. That was the name of her favorite book. Jojo even barked for them!

Collette put down the tape. She picked a photo out of the box. It was a picture of the Baker kids. They stood, crowded together on their front lawn.

"The Martians will think we're a real funny-looking family," she said. "I mean, look at us. Jack and I are African-American. Mark is Korean. You and Kenny are Puerto Rican. Then there're Kevin and Patty with red hair. Terry and Dixie are blondes. Except Dixie's hair is stick straight, and Terry's a curly-head. Hilary, Chris, and Howie have dark hair but light skin. We look all mixed up."

"That's why this is perfect," Olivia explained. "It will show them that there are all kinds of people on the planet Earth."

Olivia looked up from the photo. "I don't think you should call the space people Martians," she said seriously. "Some scientists thought they saw canals up there through their telescopes, but when they sent up the Viking satellites to take pictures, they didn't find anybody."

"Sorry," said Collette. "I didn't mean to offend space people or anything."

"It's okay," said Olivia. "There might have been life on Mars once. Maybe they built the canals and then went to another planet. It's possible."

"Yeah," said Collette, beginning to put her hair into the braid she usually wore. "Maybe they even came to Earth way long ago. Maybe we're Martian children. Or maybe we're all different colors because we're from a bunch of different planets. Oh, man, what a cool idea!"

Olivia frowned. "Anything is possible, I

suppose. But if we were from different planets, we'd be much more different than we are. We are all definitely humanoids."

"I still say it's a cool idea," Collette insisted. "What else have you got?"

Olivia pulled the rest of the things from her box. There was an *X-Men* comic, a *TV Guide*, and a picture of Sally Ride that Olivia had cut out from her school newsletter.

Chris had donated her Barbie doll, which she no longer played with now that she was sixteen. Collette lifted the doll tenderly. "Are you sure you want to put this in the box?" she asked. "It's such a nice one."

"Don't worry," laughed Olivia. "It's not really going into space. It's just a science project." She took a piece of white paper from the box and handed it to Collette. "Jack gave me this to put in the box," she said.

Collette unfolded the paper. She chuckled when she saw the crayon drawing.

8

"Pretty good for a five-year-old," she said. Jack had drawn a picture of a very small astronaut. "But what are these blue dots over his head?" asked Collette.

"Those are tears," Olivia told her. "There's a story on the back. Jack told it to Mom and she wrote it down for him."

Collette turned the paper over and read the story, which was written in blue crayon. It said:

My big sister Olivia is going to be an astronaut. You have to be big to be an astronaut. A little kid couldn't be an astronaut. If the little kid went away on a long trip to space, he would miss his mom and dad too much. Then he would cry and cry. There is no gravity in space. So his tears would float over his head and get all over the place. The end.

Collette grinned, then she grew serious. "Are you showing this drawing to the class?" she asked.

"It's about space," said Olivia. "Do you think it's dumb?"

"I think it's cute. But Bobby Wernick and his stupid pals might think it was dumb," Collette pointed out.

Bobby Wernick was the biggest pain in Ms. Sherman's third grade. He worshipped the fifth-grade bully, Snoddy Goldleaf, and tried to be just like him. His greatest thrill was when Snoddy paid attention to him.

A small group of boys hung around with Bobby. They laughed at everything he said.

Snoddy Goldleaf picked on everyone. And that included the Baker kids. But Bobby Wernick had his own special reason for picking on the Bakers.

Bobby hated the Bakers because his father hated them.

At one time, Mr. Wernick had tried to force the Bakers to move. He said it wasn't natural for a family to be different colors.

Mr. Wernick even told people that the Bakers weren't really a family. He said they were running an illegal orphanage. He even got a small group of people to sign a petition saying they didn't want to have the Bakers in their neighborhood.

Of course, it was all a lie. Mr. Wernick really wanted the Bakers out because all the Baker kids were not white. Mr. and Mrs. Baker didn't let Mr. Wernick get away with it. They went and talked to every person who had signed the petition. "We are a real family," Mr. Baker assured them. When the people met the Bakers, many of them changed their minds. At the next town meeting, some of them called Mr. Wernick a troublemaker. No one ever spoke about the Bakers moving again.

But Mr. Wernick continued to hate the Bakers. Through the years the Bakers adopted more and more kids. Each time they did, Mr. Wernick tried to spread nasty gossip about them. By then it didn't matter. Nobody listened to Mr. Wernick anymore.

"Do you think Bobby and his friends will make fun of my project?" Olivia asked Collette.

Collette wrinkled her nose. "You know what creeps they are," she replied. "They might."

Olivia picked up her box and stood. "Well, I don't care," she said firmly. But that wasn't true. She did care.

2

Enemies

TWO WEEKS AGO Bobby Wernick had made a discovery that made life very difficult for Olivia. He had discovered he could make Olivia cry.

Olivia wasn't a sissy. Not at all. In fact, she was always ready to stand up for herself or a friend, or one of her brothers or sisters.

But she *did* cry easily.

Olivia cried at sad movies, over sad books, even over sad songs. Her dark eyes misted up when she saw a dead animal in the road. She cried so hard during *E.T.* that her glasses fogged. The family had to put the VCR on *pause* until her tears dried.

Two weeks ago Bobby had been teasing little Jack in the schoolyard. He took Jack's lunch bag and held it high over his head. Olivia saw this and rushed over. "Leave him alone!"

"Ha! Ha! Now you're going to get it!" Jack shouted at Bobby.

Olivia grabbed for the bag, but Bobby jerked it away. "Give it to me," she insisted.

Bobby held out the bag. As Olivia reached for it, he pulled it back again. "What's the matter, four-eyes, can't you see the bag?" he taunted. "What are you? Blind?"

"Don't call me four-eyes," said Olivia angrily. She grabbed for the bag, and this time she got it. But Bobby was fast, too. He reached out and pulled off her glasses. "Now you don't have four-eyes anymore," he jeered as he tossed the glasses against the schoolyard fence.

That was when Olivia started to cry.

"What a baby! Crybaby Baker! Crybaby Baker!" Bobby chanted. A group of Bobby's friends came over. One of them was named Harry Schneider. In the first and second grade Harry and Olivia had been friends. Then Harry started hanging out with Bobby and stopped being friends with Olivia.

Olivia saw the boys snickering at her. One of the boys whispered something to Harry, and he laughed.

"Come on," Olivia said, taking Jack's hand as she walked toward her glasses. She knelt and picked up the glasses. The frame was cracked on one side.

"Don't cry," said Jack, patting her shoulder soothingly.

"What happened?" asked Mr. Popol, one of the third-grade teachers.

Normally, Olivia didn't tattle. But this

time she was mad. "Bobby Wernick threw them," she said, wiping her eyes.

"He stole my lunch, too," Jack added. "He wouldn't give it back, but Olivia got it."

Mr. Popol's mouth turned into a thin angry line. He walked over to Bobby, grasped his shoulder tightly, and led him into the building. Olivia was pretty sure they were going to see Mrs. Nardone, the principal.

Ever since that day, Bobby made Olivia his special target. He'd hiss "Crybaby! Crybaby!" whenever she passed. Even though she turned her head and tried to ignore him, his words hurt and embarrassed her.

What was worse, Harry Schneider would laugh right along with the other boys. Before, Olivia hadn't understood why he had stopped being her friend. Now he had really become her enemy.

On the morning her science project was due, Olivia tried not to worry about Bobby or Harry. Her project was too important to her. It didn't matter what some dumb boys thought.

Olivia gave her presentation right after attendance. She stood in front of the class. Her space box sat on Ms. Sherman's desk.

Collette, Hilary, and Patty all had Ms. Sherman for a third-grade teacher. They'd already presented their projects a few days before.

Collette sat up straight and smiled at Olivia. Patty put her fingers under her chin and waved hi. Hilary crossed her eyes and quickly darted her tongue out.

"Go ahead, Olivia," said Ms. Sherman, seated at the back of the class.

Olivia showed the class her box and explained what it was. "NASA really sent things like this into space," she told the class.

Hilary raised her hand. "What's NASA?" she asked, tossing back her long brown hair.

Olivia was prepared for this question.

In fact, she'd told Hilary to ask it — just in case anyone in the class needed to know. "NASA is a short way of saying National Aeronautics and Space Administration," Olivia explained.

"Thank you, that's extremely interesting," said Hilary.

"NASA sent up lots of things for space people to find," Olivia continued, feeling more relaxed. "They put them in unmanned satellites." She talked to the class about some of those things, like the whale sounds and the samples of many different languages.

Then she presented the contents of her box. "These are the things I would send," she said. In the morning, she had made two additions to her box. She'd added a plastic bag full of Tang orange drink. The astronauts had drunk it in space on some of the missions. It was Olivia's favorite drink. "Maybe space people would like to try it," she said.

She had also put in a pack of begonia

seeds. "These probably wouldn't grow on any of the planets in our solar system," she explained. "But a satellite like *Voyager 2* — which left our solar system in nineteen eighty-nine — might reach a planet in another solar system that is just like Earth. Years and years from now, our great-great-grandchildren might find begonias there — the begonias we sent. You never know."

"Ha!" Bobby scoffed in a low voice that everyone around him could hear. "That's so dumb!" He wore a smirky smile.

Olivia didn't look at him again. *He's just a jerk,* she told herself. But she decided not to take Jack's drawing from the box. It was too sweet a thing to let Bobby and his friends make fun of.

Olivia played the tape she'd made. Some of the kids giggled when the toilet flushed. When Dixie spoke, the girls said, "Ah," and "How cute." The class seemed to like the tape.

"Even the government of the United

States thinks we might hear from space people some day. They have a project called SETI — Search for Extra-Terrestrial Intelligence," she told the class. Olivia had discovered this fact while researching her project.

"You mean like E.T.?" Vinnie O'Neil called out.

Olivia nodded. "That's what E.T. stands for. Extra-Terrestrial."

"Wow! Cool!" said Vinnie.

"They will be listening for radio waves from outer space," Olivia went on. "Some people think this is a waste of time, but I disagree. I think that if they listen long enough, they *will* hear from somebody out there." Olivia paused and looked at Ms. Sherman. "That's the end."

Ms. Sherman clapped. "Excellent, Olivia," she said. The class clapped, too. Ms. Sherman walked toward the front of the room. "I should mention that no one has ever proven that there are other people out in space," she told the class. "There could be, but we're not sure."

"I'm sure," said Olivia.

"Yeah, because you're one of them," Bobby shouted.

Ms. Sherman shot him a warning glance.

Patty, Hilary, and Collette glared. A small ripple of laughter ran through the class.

Olivia could feel herself blush, but she held her head high. "No," she said. "I think that because it makes sense. We know other planets revolve around other suns. So, there is probably a planet out there that is as far from its sun as we are from our sun. Or, maybe other kinds of life exist that don't need the same conditions we do. Anyway, I guess to those extra-terrestrials, *you're* the alien."

"Ha, ha, slobby Bobby, I guess that will shut you up," laughed Collette.

Ms. Sherman clapped her hands. "Bobby! Collette!"

Olivia took her seat. Alice Birmingham

presented her project next. She'd made a volcano from papier-mâché. She was about to make it erupt.

Suddenly, someone tossed a folded note onto Olivia's desk. It came from Ellie Pringle, the girl behind Olivia. "Who's this from?" Olivia whispered to Ellie.

"I don't know," Ellie whispered back.

Olivia unfolded the note. She knew right away that it came from Bobby. It was a picture of a space creature. There were four big eyes on the face, and horns coming out of the head. It said: *Olivia the four-eyed creature*.

Crumpling the paper, Olivia tossed it inside her desk.

3

A Strange Visit

THAT AFTERNOON, OLIVIA sat in her room doing her math homework. She knew it would take a lot of education to become an astronaut. Even after college she would have to keep going to school. That was okay if it would get her into outer space.

Across the room, Collette lay on her bunk tearing pictures out of a magazine. She was working on a new project Ms. Sherman had assigned. Each student had to make a collage showing what she imagined her life would be like as a grown-up.

"Here," said Collette, holding up a magazine picture. "This will be me when I grow up." It was a full-color car ad. A beautiful, black-skinned woman was climbing into a silver sports car in front of a mansion.

Olivia smiled. "Where are you getting all that money from?"

"I told you I'm going to be a famous artist, remember?" said Collette, who loved to draw and paint.

Suddenly Hilary burst into the room holding a magazine. "I found it!" she announced happily. "The perfect wedding dress!"

"Hilary! You never told us you were getting married!" Collette teased. "When's the big day?"

"Ha, ha, ha," said Hilary dryly. "This is for my collage. Naturally I'm going to be a bride. And this is the dress I'll wear."

"Is that *all* you want to be?" asked Olivia. "A bride?"

"Of course not," Hilary replied, lifting

her slightly pointy nose. "I want to be a ballerina, too. And a movie star."

"Hilary!" cried Patty, stomping angrily into the room. "Give me my magazine. I know you took it off my bed."

"Well, excuse me, but I found this great wedding dress," said Hilary, lifting the magazine to show Patty.

"Sally Ride got married in jeans and a rugby shirt," Olivia told them. She'd read this in a magazine article about the astronaut.

"Oh! Yick!" groaned Hilary. "Why did she do that?"

"She was in a hurry to get back to work."

Chris came to the open doorway. She was sixteen and her dark curly hair was tied up high on her head. Her brown eyes were rimmed with eyeliner. "Oh, Olivia," she said in a teasing, singsong voice. "There's someone at the front door to see you. A boy."

"A boy!" cried Hilary excitedly. "Who?"

"Harry Schneider."

The girls looked at one another with troubled expressions. "What is *he* doing here?" asked Patty.

"He's looking for trouble," Collette decided, getting up from her bed. "I'll go tell him to get lost."

"I'm coming with you," said Hilary.

"Whoa!" said Chris, stopping them at the door. "He asked for Olivia. Want me to get rid of him, Olivia?"

Olivia fiddled nervously with her pencil. "I guess I'll go see what he wants," she said. "I'm kind of curious."

Olivia headed down the hallway. From the top of the stairs, she saw Harry standing by the door. He had lots of dark brown hair, bright green eyes, and freckles.

"Hi," he said as Olivia came down the stairs.

"Hi. What's up?" she asked.

Harry studied his boots. "I hope you don't think this is weird, but I really liked your report today. I was wondering if you could tell me more about your project."

Olivia remembered that Harry used to like space a lot. One of their favorite games had been pretending they were exploring a new planet together. They would walk around the yard with water pistols (imagining they were ray guns) and pretend to discover amazing new life-forms.

"I thought you didn't like that stuff anymore," she said.

Harry shrugged. "Well, I still do."

At that moment, Mrs. Baker came in the front door. She wore a red hat and a flowing blue cape that covered her round belly. Mrs. Baker was expecting a baby. With her were Dixie and Jack. "Hello, Harry," Mrs. Baker said pleasantly, pulling off her hat and letting her blonde hair fall to her shoulders. "We haven't seen you around here for a while now. How are you?"

"Fine," Harry said, looking uncomfortable.

"Don't just stand there," said Mrs. Baker. "Come on in and sit in the living room. We'll make you some lemonade."

Harry followed Mrs. Baker into the living room. Olivia hadn't decided if she wanted Harry to stay. Now it looked as though she was stuck with him. "I'll go get my project," she said, running upstairs.

"Did you get rid of him?" asked Collette when Olivia came into the room.

Olivia shook her head. "Mom invited him in for lemonade."

"Oh, no," Patty groaned.

"He says he wants to see my project again," said Olivia, taking her space box from under her bed. "I'll just show it to him and then tell him to go."

"This is too bizarre," stated Hilary. "Why would he want to be your friend again after all this time?"

"I don't know," Olivia admitted as she left the room.

Downstairs, Olivia joined Harry on the worn blue couch. "What part of the project do you want to see?" she asked, holding the box on her lap.

Harry seemed nervous. He sipped the drink Mrs. Baker had given him. His hands shook, and he didn't look at Olivia. "I'm interested in the way the aliens will contact us," he said. "How do you think they'll do it?"

"We might receive a radio signal that is a series of beeps," she told him. "The scientists would be able to tell if the beeps were something in nature, or if intelligent beings were sending them. I read that in a book by Carl Sagan — you know, the scientist who comes on TV sometimes."

"I don't watch a lot of science shows," said Harry.

"I thought you were still interested in science," Olivia questioned.

"Oh, I am," Harry said quickly. "I just didn't see the Carl Sagan ones. But I watch all the other things about space all the time."

"Oh," said Olivia.

"Tell me more about the codes," said Harry. "I'm really interested in that."

"The most interesting thing that NASA has done is send a math code that makes a picture," Olivia went on. "I don't really understand how the code works. They sent it by radio signal, and it formed the picture of a person. Then space people would know what we look like."

"Cool," said Harry, not seeming nervous any longer.

Suddenly, Olivia had the feeling someone was watching her. She looked up and saw Patty, Hilary, and Collette crowded at the top of the stairs, peeking over the banister. Harry looked up and saw them, too.

The girls glared at Harry.

Harry blushed red as a strawberry. He folded and unfolded his hands.

"They don't trust you," Olivia said, getting up. "Harry, why did you come over? Really?"

"I don't know. I mean, we used to be friends and all."

A small fluttery happy feeling came up inside Olivia. Did Harry want to be friends again? She hoped so.

Olivia looked back at the stairs. Her sisters were still glaring. "It's okay," she told them. "Everything's okay."

With one last glare at Harry, the girls turned and went back upstairs.

"I have some books on space in the den," Olivia told Harry. "One has neat pictures of Jupiter. The *Voyager 2* satellite sent them back."

"You mean *real*, actual pictures?" said Harry.

"Sure. Come on, I'll show you." Olivia led Harry to the den. They were greeted by the sight of seven-year-old Howie twirling in the middle of the room.

"This is Space Station Baker! Come in, Ground Central!" Howie shouted, pushing his glasses up on his nose as he spun. "The moon monsters are spinning us out of control."

A six-year-old boy with red hair and freckles popped out from behind the TV. "Ground Central can't help you!" cried six-year-old Kevin. "We moon monsters have taken over Space Station Baker."

Kevin jumped on Howie, knocking him over. "I gotcha! Gotcha!"

"Ouch! That hurt!" Howie grunted, lying flat on the rug.

"Hey, guys, Mom is looking for you," said Olivia. "She said something about taking baths."

Both boys sat up straight, their eyes wide with alarm. "Time to zoom home from Space Station Baker," said Howie dramatically. "We must return to Earth and become silent ninjas."

Kevin nodded and put his finger to his lips. Together the boys slipped out of the room. "That was a fib," Olivia admitted to Harry. "But it was the only way I could get rid of them. They'll spend the next hour hiding around the house. They hate baths."

Harry smiled. Olivia took the books from the den shelf. She and Harry sat on the floor looking through them.

At five-thirty Mr. Baker came into the den. He was a tall man with thin, wispy blond hair. "Harry, your mother is here to pick you up," he said.

Harry got up. "Thanks for showing me this stuff, Olivia," he said. "I had fun."

"Me, too," said Olivia. As Olivia put the books away, she wondered why a nice kid like Harry Schneider was hanging around with a creep like Bobby Wernick.

4

Private Thoughts

THAT NIGHT, AFTER SUPPER, Olivia worked on her collage. She was alone in her room. Collette and Terry were downstairs watching TV.

Carefully, Olivia laid out the magazine pictures on her bed. She had a picture of a rocket ship taking off, and a picture of the moon.

NASA hoped to have a manned space station on the moon by the year 2000. Olivia planned to live on that space station.

Another picture was of a giant radio

dish. She'd gotten it from a science magazine. It was the largest dish in the world, and it was in Puerto Rico. Scientists had used the dish to send messages into space. They were hoping to contact other life — even though the radio waves might take billions of years to reach anyone.

If they got a message back, that dish at Arecibo Observatory, in Puerto Rico, would receive it.

Puerto Rico. Olivia had never been there. But her natural parents were Puerto Rican, though they lived in New York City.

A social worker told Olivia that her natural mother had been no more than a teenager. She'd brought Olivia to the Foundling Hospital when she was a baby. Olivia's mother told the people there that she wasn't able to take care of Olivia. She was too young and too poor.

That was the official story. But Olivia had another idea that she liked better.

Olivia sometimes imagined that she was

a child from outer space. Perhaps a passing ship had dropped her off. Or maybe the teenager who was supposed to be her natural mother had simply been walking on the roof one evening when she saw a bundle drifting down on a parachute. The bundle was Olivia.

It was a scene Olivia imagined over and over. For some reason, it was always sunset. The sky was orange and pink. She imagined the young girl who was supposed to be her natural mother wondering where Olivia had come from. Her mother never told anyone about this because — after all — who would believe her? And being so young herself, her mother had no choice but to give her to the Foundling Hospital.

Of course, Olivia had no strange powers. And she looked like a human girl. But maybe space people were just like Earth people.

Olivia had never told this story to anyone. Not even to Collette, her closest friend. For one thing, Olivia knew it wasn't true. It was just a daydream that she enjoyed.

One thing Olivia knew for sure. She wanted to go into space so much that sometimes her heart ached. The planets and stars were just so beautiful and mysterious. And certainly there were other people out there. People with so much to tell.

Olivia didn't understand why *everyone* on Earth wasn't dying to travel through space.

Something halfway under Collette's bed caught Olivia's eye. It was the magazine Hilary had brought into the room, and it was still opened to the page with the bridal gown.

That was just like Hilary. One minute she would get all excited about something. The next minute she'd leave it forgotten under a bed somewhere.

Olivia hopped off the bed and went to pick up the magazine. The gown *was* pretty. It made Olivia think again about being married in a pair of jeans. Maybe she didn't have to be like Sally Ride in *every* way.

Sally Ride had married another astronaut. He'd gone up on a space shuttle mission after Sally went. *What great talks they must have!* thought Olivia.

Harry Schneider liked space. Did he want to be an astronaut? For a moment, Olivia pictured the two of them floating among the stars in their space suits.

"Don't be dumb," Olivia scolded herself, and went back to working on her collage.

Just then she heard the front door open and close downstairs. Mr. and Mrs. Baker had gone to a town meeting after supper. Olivia and all the other Baker kids always liked to hear about the meetings. It seemed something interesting always happened.

Olivia put down her collage and headed to the den. When she neared the stairs she could hear her father's voice. It sounded angry. "I don't believe that guy. Someday I'm going to punch him right in the nose."

"Tom, you wouldn't!" gasped Mrs. Baker.

"No, I wouldn't," Mr. Baker admitted. "But I would sure *like* to."

"Hey, Dad, who are you going to hit?" twelve-year-old Mark asked excitedly, running in from the kitchen.

"What happened?" Olivia asked as she came down from the stairs.

"No one," Mrs. Baker said firmly. "Your father is not hitting anyone."

"It's that idiot John Wernick," explained Mr. Baker, settling down on the living room couch. "He wants the town to stop Sid Arthur from putting a for sale sign on his lawn."

The younger Baker kids were already sleeping. The older kids came into the living room from all corners of the house. "Why should that bother him?" asked Chris.

"Because then anyone who sees the sign can stop and offer to buy the house," said Mrs. Baker.

"So?" asked Kenny. "What's wrong with that?"

"Wernick wants every house that's sold in Wild Falls to be sold privately through the Argate Real Estate Agency," said Mr. Baker.

"Which his brother happens to own," added Mrs. Baker.

"That way Wernick can make sure only someone he approves of will buy a house in his neighborhood," Mr. Baker continued.

"How can he do that?" asked Hilary, who came in with her hair in electric rollers.

"Only people the Wernicks approve of would get to hear about the house that is for sale," said Mrs. Baker.

"That's illegal!" Chris exploded.

"Who doesn't Wernick approve of?" asked Collette.

Mr. and Mrs. Baker looked at one another sadly. "Mr. Wernick doesn't approve of anyone who isn't as white as he is," Mr. Baker said after a moment.

"What a creep," muttered Patty.

Suddenly Mrs. Baker smiled. "You should have seen your father, though. He was great. He stood up and called Wernick a . . . oh what was it? . . . A buffoon. A blowhard. And a pernicious bigot."

"Is that bad?" asked Hilary, scrunching up her mouth in a confused expression.

"A buffoon is a fool," Mr. Baker said. "A blowhard is full of big talk with no real backing. Pernicious means destructive. And bigots are people who can't tolerate anyone who is different from themselves."

"I guess you don't like the guy," chuckled Mark as he sat on the floor petting Jojo. "What did he do when you called him those things?"

Mrs. Baker laughed. "He turned bright red. He was so mad, he couldn't even reply. Almost everyone in the room clapped and cheered for your father."

"Way to go, Dad!" cheered Kenny.

Mr. Baker smiled, but his eyes were sad. "I don't understand people like him. Why waste your energy hating like that?"

Olivia listened as the family talked about the rest of the meeting. She wondered if Mr. Wernick were home talking to his family in the same way the Bakers were talking. He was probably saying awful things about them.

Quietly, Olivia sighed. She was proud of her father, but she wondered if she should expect trouble from Bobby on Monday. Something told her she should.

5

Something Silver

THE WEEKEND PASSED quickly. The kids
spent Saturday helping Miss Peabody, the
housekeeper, clean up. On Sunday, they
went to Grannie Baker's house. She
cooked them a feast of different Chinese
dishes. She'd learned to cook Chinese food
during her trip to China.

Monday was so rainy that the kids
couldn't play in the schoolyard before
class. They had to go inside to the lunchroom.

Olivia walked down the wide cafeteria steps alongside Patty, Hilary, Collette, and Kenny. "Don't look now, but look who's there," said Collette in a low voice.

Bobby Wernick and his friends — Denny Adams, Corey Myers, Don Pennetti, and Harry Schneider — stood by the door. All of them but Harry wore mean little smiles on their faces. Harry just stared at the ceiling.

"Ignore them," said Hilary.

But it was impossible to ignore them. As they passed, Bobby whispered, "One, two, three." All at once the boys cried out, "Help! It's Four-Eyed Olivia, the nerd from outer space! We're being attacked by space nerds! Help!"

In the lunchroom, kids stopped talking and stared at them. Olivia felt the hot tingle of tears starting up. *Don't cry,* she commanded herself. *Whatever happens, don't cry!* She looked at Harry. He wasn't shouting, but he was still standing with his friends.

Harry had stopped staring at the ceiling. Now he studied his boots.

"Hey, Wernick, I'm going to make your face funnier than it already is," cried Kenny.

"Yeah, and I'll help him," added Collette.

"I'm so scared, I'm shivering," jeered Bobby.

"You should be," Hilary shouted, standing behind Collette.

"Ooooh, ooh! The Baker nerds are going to hurt me. I'm *soooo* scared," Bobby taunted.

In the next second, Kenny jumped on Bobby, knocking him to the ground. Don Pennetti jumped on top of Kenny. Collette wrapped her hands around Don's forehead and yanked him backward off Kenny.

Tweeeeeeeeeeeeet! A piercing whistle blasted the air, and a short woman with tight, orange curls charged across the cafeteria.

"Uh-oh. Mrs. Arnold," said Olivia. Mrs. Arnold was the head of the lunchroom. And she was the meanest woman in the whole school.

Kenny, Bobby, and Collette scrambled to their feet. "He hit me," Bobby told Mrs. Arnold.

"He was bugging my sister," Kenny defended himself.

"Our sister didn't say a word to him," added Collette. "He was picking on her."

Mrs. Arnold peered down at them, her hands on her hips. She had very white skin and beady blue eyes. Although she was small for an adult, she somehow managed to seem very large. "Time to visit Mrs. Nardone," she said. "March!"

When Mrs. Arnold said "March!" — kids marched. Bobby, Kenny, and Collette walked out the door with Mrs. Arnold close behind. Corey, Denny, Don, and Harry all rushed off in the other direction.

"I feel terrible," Olivia said to Patty and Hilary.

"It's not your fault," said Patty. "It's jerky Wernick's fault. What a moron!"

"I bet he did this because of what happened at the town meeting," said Hilary. "He's probably mad because our father called his father all those B things."

"I can't believe Harry Schneider!" Patty added. "And you were so nice to him on Friday, too!"

A lump rose in Olivia's throat. Why had Harry been so mean? She had thought they were friends again.

For the rest of the day, Olivia felt gloomy. She slumped in her desk, her chin on her hand.

Harry sat toward the front of the class. Olivia couldn't stop staring at the back of his head. Once, he turned and looked at her. Then he turned back quickly.

Ellie Pringle passed a note to Olivia. It was from Patty. She'd drawn a picture of Harry with arrows through his head. The picture was so silly, it made Olivia feel a little better.

"Now, class, I have something important to tell you," announced Ms. Sherman. Olivia crumpled the note and sat up. "I have decided which two science projects will be sent down to the school science fair. As you know, only two projects from each class are allowed. It was a difficult decision, but Estelle Laskin and Olivia Baker will be going on to the science fair."

Ms. Sherman clapped. The rest of the class clapped, too. For the first time all day, Olivia smiled.

That evening, the family sat down to eat at the long kitchen table. Mr. Baker clinked his glass with his fork. "Quiet, please," he said. Slowly, everyone stopped talking. "I want to congratulate Olivia on having her science project chosen for the science fair," he said, raising his glass.

"Hooray, hooray!" the kids cheered.

"Thanks," said Olivia, smiling brightly.

"We know someday you'll be a great astronaut," added Mrs. Baker as she cut up Dixie's meat.

"I hope you'll all come visit me on the moon," said Olivia.

"Cool, man," said twelve-year-old Mark. "I can just see me packing my bags and saying, 'So long, I'm going to the moon to see my little sister.'"

"Can you imagine twelve Baker kids on the moon?" laughed Chris. "It really *would* be Space Station Baker."

"Thirteen kids," said Mrs. Baker, patting her round belly. "You'll have a baker's dozen on the moon."

Long ago, bakers gave one roll free if you bought twelve rolls. Thirteen of anything came to be known as a baker's dozen. Now that the Baker family was expecting their thirteenth child, they liked to say they were a real Baker's dozen.

"How do you know about Space Station Baker?" Howie asked Chris.

"How could I not know?" laughed Chris. "You were yelling, 'Come in, Space Station Baker,' all over the house."

"Oh," said Howie.

After the kitchen was cleaned, Olivia helped Kenny with his punishment home-work. Collette had already done hers. They had to write "I must not fight in the lunchroom" a hundred times.

"Uh-oh," said Kenny when they were halfway done. "Our writing doesn't look the same. Yours is neat, and mine is . . . well . . . sort of sloppy."

Olivia studied the two sets of writing. "We'll put mine first and yours last," she suggested. "You can say your hand got tired toward the end."

Kenny smiled. "Good idea," he said. Kenny's dark eyes grew serious. "What we're writing is a lie. I'll pop Bobby again tomorrow if he bugs you."

"Those guys are just idiots," said Olivia glumly.

That night, Olivia was so excited about going to the science fair that she couldn't sleep. Lying in bed, she thought up ways to improve her project.

A round, white moon sat in the sky. It threw bright beams into the dark room. Olivia got out of bed and softly padded across the floor to the window.

She gazed up at the moon for a while, not thinking much of anything — just looking. Then her eyes traveled down to the yard below. Rows of flowers were planted in a little garden. The trees swayed gently in the breeze.

Suddenly, Olivia noticed something silvery dangling from the branch of the big oak closest to the yard. What could it be?

She ran back to the nightstand, got her glasses, and looked out the window again. The object was still there, but she couldn't tell what it was. *Strange,* she thought. She'd been in the yard that evening, helping Mark bring out the garbage. She hadn't noticed it then.

Who could have put it there? In the morning, she would have to check.

Olivia got back into bed and tried to

sleep. She turned to her right. She turned to her left. She flipped over onto her stomach.

It was useless.

Restlessly, Olivia walked back to the window. The silver thing still danced in the wind. *As long as I can't sleep,* thought Olivia, *I might as well go down and see what that stupid thing is.*

6

The Message

OLIVIA STOOD IN THE FRONT HALL and pulled on her sneakers. Her blue denim jacket was zipped up over her nightgown.

The house was quiet except for the *tick . . . tick . . . tick . . .* of the clock in the living room.

Squeeech, squeech! The rubber soles of her sneakers made noise as she headed for the kitchen. Why did the littlest sound seem so loud late at night? she wondered.

The bright moon sent lines of silver wavering across the kitchen floor. Olivia opened the back door and went out into the yard. She jammed her hands into her pockets and ran out toward the trees.

There it was. The silver thing hung from a branch just above her head. Olivia jumped once. Twice. On the third try she grabbed it. One sharp yank broke the silver ribbon that tied it to the tree.

It was a bag. Shiny, smooth, and cold. It was tied into a knot at the top. Olivia tried to undo the knot, but it was too tight. Clutching the bag, she hurried back to the house.

In the kitchen, Olivia used a small knife to unknot the bag. Inside she found a plain white card with numbers on it. The numbers were neatly done in a dark ink. Who had tied this to the tree? And why?

By the light of the moon, Olivia studied the numbers. They didn't seem to be in any order at all.

7 18 5 5 20 9 14 7 19
5 1 18 20 8 12 9 14 7

```
23  1  20  3  8
6  15  18
19  9  7  14  1  12
13  21  19  20
13  1  11  5
3  15  14  20  1  3  20
21  18  7  5  14  20
```

Olivia stared and stared at the numbers. "I don't get it," she mumbled. "What could — "

Suddenly the kitchen light snapped on. "What are you doing?" asked Collette, her blue terry robe wrapped tightly around her. "I woke up and saw you weren't in your bed and — "

"Come here, look at this," said Olivia.

Collette sat beside Olivia at the table. "Weird bag," she noted, smoothing out the silver bag.

"This card was inside the bag, and the bag was tied to a tree," Olivia explained. "What do you think it means?"

Collette looked at the card. "It means

. . . it means . . . it means some math nut is running around out in the woods." Collette turned the card in her hand. "I don't *believe* you went out in the middle of the night to get this. Who would do such a nutty thing?"

"I don't know," replied Olivia. "It's got to be a code of some kind."

The two girls stared at the card. "This is totally strange," Collette commented.

Olivia studied the code. Suddenly she had an idea. "I think this is written in an alphabet code."

"Are you sure?" asked Collette.

"Let's see," said Olivia. "The first number is seven. That would be equal to G, the seventh letter of the alphabet. The next number is 18. That would equal . . ." Silently Olivia counted through the alphabet, using her fingers to keep track. "It equals R!"

Collette got up and fished through the family's odds-and-ends drawer. She found a notepad and a broken pencil. First she wrote out the alphabet, then she put the numbers one through twenty-six above each letter.

"Let me have it," said Olivia excitedly. Taking the pencil from Collette, she began to work on the code. "Oh, my gosh!" she gasped as she wrote. *"Ohmygoshohmygooooo-sshhhhhh!"*

"What?" asked Collette. "What is it?"

"The first two words spell, 'Greetings, Earthling'," said Olivia, her eyes ablaze with excitement. "Collette, this is a message from outer space!"

"No!" said Collette in amazement.

"Sure, sure. It's got to be," said Olivia. "This is so great. This is *soooooooooooo* great!"

"Well, what else do they have to say?" Collette asked impatiently.

Olivia continued to work feverishly on the note. It wasn't long before she had decoded the entire message: *Greetings, Earthling. Watch for signal. Must make contact. Urgent.*

"This is unbelievable," said Olivia, looking stunned. "I've been contacted by an alien!"

"Are you positive?" asked Collette gently.

Olivia walked to the kitchen window and looked out at the bright moon. "Of course, I'm positive. What other explanation could there be?"

Collette just looked at Olivia.

Olivia's shoulders sagged. "I suppose there could be lots of other explanations," she admitted. "In fact, I don't think an alien would use an alphabet code. If they already knew the alphabet, there would be no reason to use a code."

"Hmmmmmmm," mused Collette, folding her arms. "Then who did leave this?"

"Yeah, who?" agreed Olivia, nodding. "And why?"

7

Alien Watch

ALL DAY SATURDAY OLIVIA kept peeking out the windows. She was waiting to see if anyone tried to contact her. So far, nothing had happened.

"Any sign?" asked Collette when they were together in their bedroom.

"No," replied Olivia.

Collette joined Olivia at the window. The sky was almost dark, but Olivia hadn't turned on a light. The room was dark, too. "I asked everyone," Collette said. "No one put that bag there."

"You asked Howie?" said Olivia. She thought this might be part of some make-believe he and Kevin were playing.

"He said he didn't know anything about it," said Collette. "Besides, he hates climbing trees, remember? He couldn't have gotten the note up there."

"What about Kenny?" Olivia checked. "He loves to climb trees."

"It wasn't Kenny, either. I asked if he could unscramble the code, and he couldn't."

"Maybe he was faking," said Olivia.

"I can tell when Kenny is faking," Collette assured her. "No, he was really trying."

"I wish this message were real," Olivia said glumly. "I just have a feeling that it isn't."

"Me, too," Collette agreed.

From downstairs came the sound of

someone yodeling. It was Grannie Baker. She was telling them that supper was ready.

Olivia and Collette went downstairs to eat. Olivia ate as quickly as she could. She wanted to get back to the window and see if someone was going to send her a signal. She was determined to get to the bottom of this mystery.

It seemed she couldn't chew fast enough. "Here, Jojo," she whispered, holding a hunk of fried chicken under her chair. The big black dog popped up from where he lay under the table. He gobbled the chicken eagerly. The Baker kids liked fried chicken, so he wasn't getting many snacks tonight.

Soon Olivia's plate was empty. Everyone else was still eating. "Can I be excused?" she asked. "I have a stomachache."

"I don't doubt it," said Mrs. Baker, looking at Olivia's plate. "Why did you eat so fast?"

Olivia shrugged her slim shoulders. "Maybe because it was so good?" she said, thinking that might be one way to explain it.

"All right," said Mr. Baker. "You can go lie down."

Olivia hurried upstairs. She pulled a chair to the window, leaving the room dark. It would be easier to see the signal if the room was dark. Rain was coming down hard. There didn't seem to be a star in the sky. Even the moon was hidden.

Sighing deeply, Olivia hugged her knees. She really did wish this wasn't a trick. It would be so thrilling to be contacted by aliens!

Olivia's imagination ran wild. She pictured herself wandering through the woods in the rain, her flashlight piercing the darkness. Then she saw it. A crashed spaceship! A small, glowing pod sat in the middle of the wrecked ship. Olivia saw herself opening the pod. Inside was a little alien. It was the cutest thing, with large brown eyes and pointy ears.

Smiling fondly, Olivia imagined lifting the alien baby. The baby smiled at her. It was all so real.

Suddenly, a hand touched Olivia's shoulder.

"Ooooh!" Olivia yelped.

She turned and saw her mother looking down at her. "Sorry, sweetheart," Mrs. Baker said kindly. "I didn't mean to scare you. When I saw the room was dark, I thought you had fallen asleep in the chair. How's your stomach?"

"It feels better," she said.

Mrs. Baker pulled up another chair and sat beside her. "What nasty weather," she commented.

Olivia nodded. "Really yucky," she agreed. "Mom, do you think I'm strange for believing in spaceships and aliens and all?" she asked after a moment.

Mrs. Baker stroked Olivia's soft hair. "I

don't think you're strange at all. Why? Has someone made fun of your science project?"

"Just Bobby Wernick and his dumb friends," Olivia told her.

Mrs. Baker shook her head sadly. "Ignore them, if you can. What is it with that family?"

"Bobby picks on me more than anybody else," Olivia told her mother. "I think it's because I cried in front of him. You remember, I told you? When he broke my glasses."

Mrs. Baker hugged Olivia. "You're a very special kind of person, Olivia," she said. "You're someone with a vision of the future. You have a dream you want to make come true. The world needs people like you very much. But dreams scare some people. I'm not sure why. And when people are scared, they feel small. So they try to make you feel small."

"What do you mean by small?" asked Olivia.

"They try to make you feel foolish. As if your dreams are silly, and everyone else knows the right answers. That's why they laugh at you. It doesn't mean they're right, though."

"I don't like it when they laugh," Olivia admitted. "I know I shouldn't care, but it makes me feel bad anyway. Is that dumb?"

Mrs. Baker squeezed Olivia gently. "It's not dumb. It's normal to feel bad when someone is mean to you," she said. "Some people laughed when we adopted so many kids. It hurt my feelings. And then there were people like Bobby's father who tried to make us feel small and foolish. But we had a dream for our future. We saw ourselves with a big, happy family. And look how well it's turned out."

Olivia hugged her mother back. She stretched her arm across her mother's wide belly. Something jumped under her fingers. "Mom!" she cried. "I felt it. I think I felt the baby move!"

"You did," smiled Mrs. Baker. "The baby just kicked."

"Cool!" Olivia cried. "Do you love the baby yet?"

"It's funny, but I do," Mrs. Baker replied. "It's odd to love someone you can't even see."

"I love the space people, and I can't see them," Olivia said.

"Maybe it's sort of the same," Mrs. Baker agreed. She ruffled Olivia's hair. "Don't worry about your science project. It's going to be terrific."

"Mom, look at this," said Olivia as Mrs. Baker got up from her chair. She showed Mrs. Baker the coded note. "I broke the code. It says, 'Greetings, Earthling. Watch for Signal. Must make contact. Urgent.' I found it hanging on a tree."

"Someone is playing a trick on you," said Mrs. Baker. "Probably one of your brothers or sisters."

"Oh, I figured it wasn't real," said Olivia. "I was just thinking that whoever sent the message might send a signal. Then I could go out and see who it was."

"Come with me," said Mrs. Baker, taking Olivia by the hand. They went downstairs to where the family was clearing the supper dishes. "Did anyone tie this coded note to a tree?" Mrs. Baker asked the family.

The kids looked at one another. Each of them denied having done it.

"Then who did?" Olivia said, throwing up her arms.

"I know!" said Patty. "Maybe someone in the science fair did it. Maybe he wanted to scare you so you wouldn't give a good science presentation."

"Or maybe he's going to signal you on the night of the science fair so you don't go," added Mark.

The science fair was Monday night. Olivia had planned to spend Sunday improving her project. "I *was* kind of forgetting about my science project," admitted Olivia.

"Well, if that's so," said Mr. Baker as he stacked dishes into the dishwasher, "I'd say the best way to get back at this person is to go work on your science project. Make it as good as it can be."

"You're right," said Olivia. "I'm going to make this the best science project ever."

8

The Science Fair

THE SCIENCE FAIR was held in the school lunchroom. All the projects were displayed on the long lunch tables. Students from grades one through six were there. Olivia stood in front of her project — her new, improved, project.

Olivia had made a large poster to place behind the space box. It showed different facts about space travel.

On the poster was a photo of Sally Ride, a magazine drawing of the *Voyager 2* space satellite, a photo of the space shuttle, and a picture of Mr. Spock and Captain Kirk from *Star Trek*. Olivia knew that Mr. Spock and Captain Kirk weren't real, but she liked them and wanted them on her poster.

Olivia had also included one of her most special pictures. It was a small, black-and-white photo of the Russian astronaut (the Russians called them cosmonauts) Valentina Tereshkova. She had been the very first woman in space. The Russians had sent her in 1963! It wasn't so easy to find pictures of Valentina. Olivia wished she knew more about her.

Olivia had also constructed a model of a space station using round cardboard tubes from toilet tissue, gift wrap, and paper towels. Her mother let her unwind the toilet tissue and paper towels and store them in a bag. Olivia used a picture of a space station as a model. She painted it white and printed the words "Space Station Baker" in the front.

It was five-thirty in the evening. Parents

and their kids were looking at the projects. Mr. and Mrs. Baker had gotten Olivia settled and gone to look at some of the other projects. Hilary, Patty, Collette, Kenny, Terry, Howie, and Kevin had come to see the fair, too. They were over looking at Estelle Laskin's project on growing string beans under different soil conditions.

Olivia was excited, but nervous. She chewed on her thumbnail. Soon, a mother and her first-grader son came to Olivia's table. Olivia stood up straight and showed the contents of her box. Then she finished up with a little speech she had prepared the night before. "It is up to each and every one of us to keep watching the skies," she said. "Someday we might meet new beings who will tell us strange and wonderful new things."

"You mean Martians are here?" gasped the boy, looking scared.

"Not yet. At least not as far as we know," Olivia told him. "And they won't be from

Mars. But someday I bet we'll meet people from some other planet. Or our great-grandchildren will. And, don't worry. I know they'll be friendly — just like E.T." The first-grader smiled.

Olivia gave the same speech to every group who came to see her project. When she talked about someday meeting aliens, people reacted in different ways. Some looked amused, as if she were being funny. Others frowned. Some nodded in agreement.

Hilary, Kenny, Collette, and Patty came to the table. They had been trying to find out who left the note on the tree. "No luck," Kenny reported.

"I was sure it was Estelle Laskin," said Hilary. "She knows her dumb old string beans don't stand a chance."

"But she didn't do it," said Patty. "She's been at her grandmother's since Friday afternoon."

"So she claims," Hilary grumbled, casting a mean look over at Estelle Laskin.

The Baker kids left when the judges came to Olivia's table. Ms. Sherman was a judge. The principal, Mrs. Nardone, and Mr. Karl from the fifth grade were the other judges. "Hello, Olivia," Ms. Sherman said. "Your poster is very nice. Let's hear your presentation."

Olivia gave her speech. She didn't change a thing. Mrs. Nardone seemed very interested, Mr. Karl smiled, and Ms. Sherman kept nodding.

"Thank you, Olivia," said Ms. Sherman as they moved on to the next project.

Suddenly, Olivia saw Harry Schneider coming toward her. She looked the other way, but he came right up to her. "What do you want?" Olivia snapped.

"I'm sorry about the other day," he said.

"You should be," Olivia replied.

Harry opened his mouth as though he were about to say something else. Then he shut it and walked away looking sad.

By seven o'clock the judges had announced the winners. Among the third-

and fourth-graders, there were three prizes. A fourth-grader won third prize, and another fourth-grader won first prize. Olivia won second prize!

"Hurrah! Bravo!" yelled the Bakers as Olivia received her ribbon from Mrs. Nardone.

Then all the winners stood together. A man from the *Wild Falls Reporter* took their picture. It was going to appear in the paper.

Olivia felt so proud and happy! She'd done a good job. In her small way, she'd helped the space program by telling people about it.

Collette helped Olivia roll up her poster and gather her things. "What did Harry Schneider want?" Collette asked.

"To say he was sorry," Olivia told her.

Collette and Olivia looked over to where Harry stood with his mother. "He's not so tough when he doesn't have Bobby around," said Collette.

Harry's mother was talking to a teacher.

Harry seemed bored. Suddenly he noticed Collette and Olivia looking at him. He looked back at them. Then he said something to his mother and headed toward them once again.

"Let's get out of here," said Olivia. She didn't want to hear anything else Harry had to say.

Collette and Olivia hurried toward the back door. The rest of the Bakers waited there for them.

"Wait, Olivia," Harry called. "I have to tell you something important." He ran and caught up with the girls.

"Go away, Harry," said Olivia.

"It's about the coded message you got," he said.

"The message!" gasped Olivia. "Did you put it there?"

"No," said Harry. "But I know who did."

9

Kenny's Plan

THAT NIGHT, ALL THE BAKER kids gathered in Collette, Terry, and Olivia's room. They had come to talk about what Harry had told Olivia.

Bobby Wernick and Don Pennetti had left the fake alien message. They'd ridden their bikes to the Baker house, sneaked through the woods, and tied the note to the tree.

"Want to hear something really awful?" said Hilary, sitting on the floor.

"I already heard something awful," said

Howie as he hung upside down from Terry's top bunk. "I heard you singing in the shower before. It was horrible."

Hilary made a face and threw a dirty sock at him. "The awful thing is that by the time Bobby Wernick is in the fifth grade, I think he'll be a bigger creep than Snoddy Goldleaf."

"What about Harry Schneider?" said Patty. "He was in on it, too. He's the biggest creep of all."

Bobby had sent Harry to visit Olivia. He said he wouldn't hang around with Harry anymore if he didn't go. His mission was to discover which codes Olivia expected aliens to use. But Harry hadn't learned anything Bobby could use, so Bobby picked a simple alphabet code.

"Harry didn't want to do it," Olivia defended him. "He said he felt really bad about it. That's why he told me."

"Can you believe those guys could come up with such a mean plan?" said Collette. She was on her bottom bunk, her legs kicked up into a shoulder stand. "Mean and dumb."

Harry explained that there was a second part to the plan. Bobby was going to signal Olivia with a flashlight. He planned to lead her out into the woods. Denny Adams, Corey Myers, and Don Pennetti would be waiting there, wearing scary rubber masks. They were going to jump out at Olivia and try to frighten her.

"Harry told me that the only reason they didn't do it over the weekend was because of the bad weather," Olivia told them.

"Does Bobby know that Harry told you?" asked Kenny, who leaned against the door.

Olivia shook her head. "He begged me not to tell anyone. He's afraid Bobby and his friends will get him if they find out he told me. Bobby will signal me tomorrow after school. Harry told me that's the new plan. I'm not going, of course. Let them stay out all night waiting for me. It will serve them right."

"Yeah!" agreed Dixie as she pushed a yellow truck along the floor. "Serve them rice! Yuck! That will show 'em."

"Serve them gopher guts!" Jack added, looking up from his coloring. "That's even worse!"

A smile crossed Kenny's face. "I think you should go out into the woods when they signal," he said.

"Are you nuts!" Mark yelped from the top of the dresser where he was seated.

"Of course he's nuts," laughed Chris, slouched against Collette's beanbag chair. "We all know that. But he comes up with cool ideas. What are you thinking, Kenny?"

"Yeah, what?" asked Terry.

Kenny walked into the middle of the room. "I have a plan."

"Does it have ninjas in it?" asked Kevin eagerly.

Kenny thought. "It could have space ninjas."

"Hurray!" cried Kevin and Howie at once.

"Me, too! Me, too!" cried Dixie. "I want to be a space ninja."

"You're too little," said Kevin.

"No, she's not," Kenny told him.

"Let's hear the plan!" Hilary exploded.

"Okay," said Kenny. "This is what we're going to do."

10

A Problem in the Plan

EXCEPT FOR DIXIE AND JACK, the Baker kids didn't get much sleep that night. They were too busy working on Kenny's plan. As soon as Mr. and Mrs. Baker had tucked in the last kid and gone downstairs, the older kids popped right back out of bed.

There was a lot to do. Chris took charge of the costumes. Hilary and Olivia helped her poke holes in six Ping-Pong balls and draw squiggly red lines on them. "Cool space eyeballs," Olivia giggled.

Mark and Kenny worked on lighting.

They collected all the flashlights they could find in the house—big lights and small penlights. Then they taped colored pieces of cellophane over all the lenses. "Where did you get this stuff?" Mark asked, holding a piece of red cellophane in his hands.

"In the closet where Mom keeps the wrapping paper," Kenny told him. "This is going to be great!"

Collette, Terry, and Patty created sound effects. Before going to bed, they had taped the sound of the vacuum cleaner and a record playing at a fast speed.

Now they sat under Collette's quilt and played the tape back. Terry covered her ears. "Aaahhhh, it sounds too strange!" she said.

Collette and Patty grinned. "That's exactly what we want," said Patty.

Howie and Kevin were assigned a special task. They had to find three water pistols in the house. "Come, silent ninja," Howie said to Kevin as they crept out into the dark hall. "I remember seeing a pistol under the living room couch. We must use our super silence so we do not wake the parent masters."

Kevin put his fingers to his lips and followed Howie.

"What should I do next?" Olivia asked Chris.

"Just rest," said Chris. "You're the star of this show."

The next day, in school, Olivia tried to ignore Bobby and his friends. She noticed that Harry wasn't with them. She spotted him on the other side of the lunchroom sitting with a boy named Dennis Mara.

"Hey Oogle-Eyes," Bobby called when she passed him in the lunchroom. "Want to know where the scariest part of space is?"

Olivia just kept walking.

"It's the space in your head where your brains are supposed to be!" Bobby shrieked. Don, Corey, and Denny howled with laughter.

"Hey, Baker," Bobby continued. "Talked to any alien life-forms, lately — other than your family, that is?"

Olivia whirled around. "No, but I have a feeling I will be making contact very soon," she said seriously.

The boys looked at one another. Their eyes danced with laughter.

Good, thought Olivia as she walked away. *Now they think I've fallen for their stupid joke.*

As soon as the Baker kids got home from school, they went back to work on their project. "There isn't much time," warned Kenny. "We've got a lot to do before they get here."

Chris and Mark made sure Dixie, Kevin, Jack, and Olivia knew their parts. Collette made one last recording in the kitchen. She recorded the sound of the food blender whirring. Hilary sprayed wads of cotton with purple spray paint.

"What is going on?" asked Miss Peabody, the housekeeper. Mrs. Baker had gone to the doctor's office for a checkup, and Mr. Baker was still at school. The tall, sharp-featured Miss Peabody was in charge through dinner.

"Nothing," said Hilary.

"Is that so?" said Miss Peabody suspiciously.

"Not really nothing," Collette offered. "We're making costumes for a play we want to put on." They couldn't tell Miss Peabody the truth. She didn't approve of pranks.

"Well, prepare your props elsewhere," Miss Peabody ordered. "I'm about to cook dinner in here."

"Sure," said Collette, helping Hilary carry out her wet cotton. They joined the other kids in the living room.

"Remember how to find us?" Kenny asked Olivia.

"Just follow their signal, but then turn right," Olivia said, remembering what they'd agreed upon.

"We'll be waiting for you," Mark said, smiling.

At four o'clock, Olivia stood by her bedroom window, ready to go. She watched her brothers and sisters trek across the yard into the woods. Mark carried his large boom box. Patty held a cardboard box full of supplies.

The sun was low in the sky. It threw a soft pinkish glow on the bare trees.

In another five minutes, Olivia saw a light flashing in the woods. It was aimed at the house. That was it! It had to be Bobby signaling to her.

Taking her flashlight from the windowsill, Olivia flicked it on and off. She wanted them to know she was coming. She waited for an answering light. Sure enough, it came.

Olivia charged out of her room and down the steps.

"Olivia! You will fall and break your neck running down the steps like that!" boomed Miss Peabody.

"Sorry, Miss Peabody," said Olivia, slowing down.

"Where did everyone disappear to?" asked Miss Peabody, tucking a strand of her steely-gray hair back into her bun.

"Ummm . . ." Olivia had to think fast. "We're playing hide-and-seek. Everyone is outside hiding. I'm it. That's why I have to go find everyone."

"What happened to the play?"

"What play?" asked Olivia.

"The one you were all working on before."

"Oh, uh, that's done. Now we're doing hide-and-seek."

"I've never liked that game," said Miss Peabody. "Children hide in unsafe places." Miss Peabody shook her head. "I'm going out and call to the children. It's getting late. I want them all inside."

Miss Peabody headed back to the kitchen and the back door. *Oh, no!* thought Olivia. Miss Peabody would ruin everything. She had to stop her!

11

Excitement

Miss Peabody had her hand on the knob of the back door when Olivia came up with an idea.

Jojo lay lazily on the floor in the kitchen. "The kids are all hiding, Miss Peabody," Olivia said. "Jojo will be able to find them real fast. He can sniff out anything. Then I'll tell everyone to come in."

"Very well," said Miss Peabody. "But don't dawdle. Dinner will be ready soon. I've prepared my specialty, soy burgers and cabbage-wrapped cauliflower."

Uggh! thought Olivia. But she was anxious to get out. "Great," she said, "I'll tell the others."

As soon as Miss Peabody shut the back door behind her, Olivia raced out into the middle of the yard. Where was the light? Had they left?

Then it came. *Flick. Flick.* Someone was flashing a light from several yards into the woods. "Stay, Jojo," she commanded the dog as she headed out into the woods.

The light kept moving back, drawing Olivia farther and farther into the forest. It was getting darker by the minute. It wasn't easy to see.

Olivia followed the light into a small valley in the woods. On the left was a large boulder. To the right was another big rock and a giant old fallen tree. For a second, Olivia caught a glimpse of Bobby Wernick as he ducked behind the boulder to the left.

She heard a rustling sound to her right. The Bakers were taking their places behind the other rock. She remembered what Mark had told her and went to the right. "Okay, aliens, I'm here," she shouted. "I want to meet you."

Olivia heard a burst of low, snickering laughter from behind the rock where the boys were hiding.

Suddenly, to her right, a bright light snapped on. Then came the loud buzzing of the vacuum cleaner that Collette and Patty had recorded.

Two red beams of light wavered against the trees. Then two blue beams shot up.

Three small figures stepped out from behind the tree trunk. Dixie, Jack, and Kevin were dressed in long gowns. The Ping-Pong eyeballs had been glued to their faces. Hilary had fashioned fuzzy purple hair with cotton and spray paint. They wore tin foil antennae, and their faces were painted blue with makeup left over from Halloween. With the flashing lights all around them they looked as if they might truly be from another world.

"Where are you from?" asked Olivia, talking loud enough so the boys would be sure to hear.

The sound of the fast-speed songs came on as a reply.

"I don't understand," said Olivia. Kevin stepped forward and beckoned to Olivia to kneel. Then he touched her forehead, just as they had practiced. "What!" Olivia cried, pretending to be alarmed. "You have uncovered spies nearby? You are going to use your laser pistols on them?"

The three Baker kids nodded and took their water pistols from behind their backs. They aimed them at the rock where Bobby, Don, and their friends hid.

Collette turned up the volume of the tape recorder to high. *Whirrrrrrrrrrrrrrrrrrrrrrrrrr* went the blender sound.

Mark, Kenny, and Terry aimed yellow and purple lights at the rock.

"Aaaaah! Help!" Bobby Wernick was the first to run, screaming, from behind the rock. But the others were right behind him — running for their lives down toward the road.

Olivia stood and watched until they were almost out of sight.

"Aha! Ha! Ha!" crowed Howie, leaping out from behind the rock. "We did it."

"Man, did you see those guys take off?" laughed Collette.

Dixie pulled off her strange eyeballs. "Did we do good?" she asked.

"You did great," said Chris, putting a jacket around Dixie's shoulders.

"Thanks, you guys," said Olivia, smiling.

"You're welcome," said Mark, his eyes bright with laughter.

Kenny ran behind the other rock and came back with three ugly rubber masks. "They were so scared, they left these behind."

Off in the distance, Jojo barked.

"Oh, my gosh!" said Olivia. "I forgot. Miss Peabody wants us to come right in. She made cabbage-wrapped cauliflower for dinner."

All the Baker kids groaned. "Beam me up! Please!" cried Howie, looking into space. "I'd rather be captured by space monsters than eat Miss Peabody's cooking."

"I don't even care," said Olivia. "I'm in such a good mood, I don't think even cabbage-wrapped cauliflower could ruin it."

As they headed back to the house, Olivia looked up and saw a fat, three-quarter moon hanging low in the sky. *Someday,* she thought. Someday she would get up there, and even farther.

She looked to either side and saw her brothers and sisters smiling and laughing as they walked. Someday would come soon enough, she decided. Right now, it felt good to be exactly where she was. Happy and loved, right here on *Earth* Station Baker.

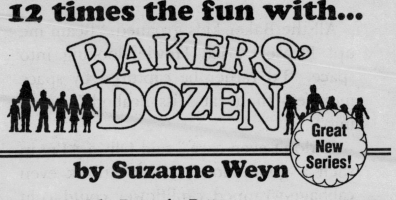